What The Darkn

By Jay

CW01660260

Copyright © 2025 Pricey Publishing

All rights reserved. No part of this book may be reproduced or transmitted in any form or by any means, electronic or mechanical, including photocopying, recording, or by any information storage and retrieval system, without written permission from the publisher

This is a work of poetry and personal reflection. Names and identifying details may have been changed.

First Edition

Dedicated to Simon Thompson
My loving Stepfather
30th March 1982- 28th May 2025

When I was thirteen my mum married again
This time to one of the most wonderful of men
He was always at the end of the phone
To come and put shelves up in my home
And never failed to remind me
I was one of his own.

Table of Contents

Foreword

Chapter One: The War Nobody Saw

The Invisible War

When The Darkness Almost Caught Me

Exhausted

10 Days

To Be or Not To Be

After The Storm

Chapter Two: A Moment of Your Time

A Moment of Your Time

Chapter Three: The Wounds I Had to Name

Genes & Queens (Part One)

Save The Tree (Part Two)

Mammy Issues

Here Where Shame Lies

The Looking Glass

Chapter Four: Worthy of the Wound

Accountability

The 'How to Be Loved' Brief

The Sun Doesn't Ask

The Price Right

Good Girl

For the Man Didn't Flinch

The Knight That Never Came

Chapter Five: A Letter to The Girl Who Needed it Most

Hindsight is a Beautiful Thing

Chapter Six: The Why Behind It All

Jacob

Rock of Gibraltar

Sparkle & Shine

While There's Still Time

Chapter Seven: Survivor's Gift

Build and They Will Come

In the Chaos, I prayed

Please God

I Still Sleep With A Night Light

My Hope Campfire

Chapter Eight The War Is Over (Well, at Least This One)

What The Darkness Taught Me

Chapter Nine: Behind The Poems

Author's Final Note

Hear It Spoken

Acknowledgements

Foreword

There was a time I didn't think I would make it out.
At the height of my battle with PMDD (Premenstrual Dysphoric Disorder), when the emotional turmoil became unbearable, I found myself standing at the edge — wondering if there was any way back.
Starting treatment felt like a betrayal of hope. I knew it would get worse before it got better, but nothing could have prepared me for just how deep the darkness would go. There were moments I genuinely feared I wouldn't survive it.

It wasn't faith in a miracle that pulled me through — it was faith in myself.
I clawed my way back, one tiny, painful step at a time. I rebuilt myself on a foundation I didn't even realise I had: resilience, stubborn hope, and a flicker of belief that even if I couldn't see the light yet, it was still there — and I was worth finding it for.

Throughout these pages, you will see me mention God. But this is not a book about religion.
This is a book about faith — whatever that looks like for you. Whether it's a higher power, the universe, love, or just the quiet, trembling voice inside that says, *keep going.*
It's about believing in something greater than your pain — but most importantly, believing in yourself.

This book isn't here to promise that life will always be easy, or that the storms will pass quickly.
It's here to offer you a way through. Not to control the weather — but to help you build the strength to weather the storm.
We can't stop bad things from happening.
But we can learn how to meet them differently — with awareness, with grace, with purpose.

This book is my offering to the world.
It started as survival. Then it became poetry. And somewhere along the way, it became a map.

You'll find poems here — but also reflections. A section called *Behind the Poems*, where I share where I was at the time of writing. Not to tell you what the poems mean — that's yours to decide — but to give context to the places they came from. My hope is that it helps you find something in them for *you.*

This isn't a book that claims to have all the answers.
But I hope it gives you better questions. I hope it holds you when things are hard. I hope it reminds you of your worth, your softness, your strength — and that you are never, ever alone.

You are still here.
And as long as you are here, there is still hope.

This is my promise to you:
My love, everything is going to be okay.

— Jay

What The Darkness Taught Me

Chapter One: The War Nobody Saw

Unbeknownst to me for a very long time, I had been battling PMDD (Premenstrual Dysphoric Disorder). In the span of six years, I survived three abusive relationships, developed an unhealthy relationship with alcohol, experienced homelessness three times, and lost a baby.

I was so caught up in chaos that it wasn't until I finally found myself in a safe enough place for the dust to settle that I could begin to recognise the pattern. Sure enough, every month—for ten days—I would sink into a deep, consuming depression.

Eventually, I was diagnosed with PMDD. For a year after the diagnosis, being strongly against contraception, I tried to manage it with kindness, preparation, and sheer determination.

But it got to a point where it was either try medication or... eventually take my own life.

I chose the medication. And I knew it might get worse before it got better. I just didn't realise how much worse.

I've endured traumas they wouldn't dare put in horror movies. And yet, no matter what's happened to me, I've always survived—some battles with more ease than others.

External battles gave my mind something to focus on—too much, perhaps. They distracted me from the darkness that had been lurking for years.

But the war in my mind? That was harder than anything that's ever *happened* to me—and that says a lot.

Still, that darkness turned out to be a strange kind of blessing. It forced me to unravel the tangled mess within myself. It made me look in the mirror and finally say: *I deserve better.*

I am truly blessed to have so many people around me who love me. But the darkness has a funny way of convincing you that you're utterly alone.

I weaponised that loneliness. In those moments when I believed I had no one, I realised something vital: only *I* could save me. And that is true for anyone. No matter who loves you, only you can save you.

For years, I longed for someone to rescue me. And whenever someone did show up claiming they could, I gave them the power to destroy me.

Without this darkness—the same darkness that almost killed me—I would not have gained the tools to become *fearless.*

So it was important to me that you see—I've earned my stripes. I don't speak from theory. I speak from the pit. From lived experience. From the days I didn't think I'd survive, and the nights I begged not to wake up.

This chapter exists as my evidence. Not for sympathy, but for credibility. I want you to know that the advice I give in this book isn't empty or abstract. It's forged from the fire I walked through.

I've resided in the same darkness you may be in right now. I've cried the same tears. I've screamed the same silent screams.

I want this book to be more than just poetry. I want it to be a map—one you can return to again and again. Outlining a journey of healing, hope, and proof that it does get better- *oh, how I promise it does get better.*

So let this chapter be a homage to the darkness. But please, don't get comfortable here. This is just a reference point—to remind you how far you've come.

This is my promise to you, my love, that everything is going to be okay.

The Invisible War

I've slayed dragons.
I've slain monsters.
I've ridden victorious from battlefields
Where the odds were against me.

But what happens
When the battle lines are in your mind?
How do you defeat the demon you cannot see?

You don't.

You get on your knees—
And pray.

When the Darkness Almost Caught Me

Something feels different about today.
I open my curtain and look through the windowpane—
Everything's grey,
Like all the colour from the world's been drained.

I glance in the mirror, and I don't look the same.
Something about me has changed,
As if someone's reached into my soul and rearranged,
And took all my glow away.

Someone closed the door
On options for me to explore,
And the only path laid before
Is—
"I don't want to be here no more."

I know it'll start to ease
If I can just find a release,
But it seems
My mind keeps me-

in a constant state of tease.

All I'm asking for is peace.
Is there a right way to say please?
What kind of fees
Do I have to pay to appease
These demons—just to let me be free?

'Cause I feel them creeping,
Tongues wagging, mouths seething,
Waiting for something to sink their teeth in.
How can I be free when
I'm struggling to breathe and—

Breathe in.
Breathe out.
Breathe in...

But part of me doesn't want to win.
Got me drowning in the deep end,
Knowing damn well I can't swim, and—
While I'm fighting depression,
I keep getting asked stupid questions:

"Are you paying into your pension?"
"Are you paying off your debt collection?"
"Are you paying attention?"

JESSICA.

"Are you paying attention?"

Turns out I still have to do the dishes
When I'd rather be sleeping with the fishes.
Turns out I still have to meet quotas
When I have a date set with my bath and toaster.

There's a blockage
That insists
On paying homage
To all the damage

That I've endured.
I have to sever this cord
Or I'm going to suffer
More and more.

I'm searching and searching,
Trying to find where this thing's lurking
Deep within—
Stopping me from winning,

Stopping me from being happy.
Happy to trap me

In a place so low—
Many a friend or even a foe
Could offer me a toe
Out of this hole.

Where is it?
I can't find it.
It's persistently hiding.
And I've stripped the walls thin,
So that means it's in the foundations and all.

Plenty of people to call,
But I can't pick up my phone—
Because I've convinced myself I'm alone,
Even if I'm not met with the dial tone.

I can't answer "What's wrong?"
Maybe I'm just tired of being strong.
Maybe all the trauma's caught up after so long.
Maybe I'm just too tired to go on.

"But why?"
They'll reply.
And all I can do is sigh,
Say "I'm just tired,"
Hang up, and cry.

It's too dark in here,
And all I seem to be able to do is shed tears.
It's when I can no longer cry that I fear—
That the end may finally be near.

Exhausted

I've not done enough today
To deserve the hours I want to sleep away.
In my dreams, I find an escape
But always seem to awake to the daunting fate
That everything must remain.
Maybe that's why I make home in pain—
Years it took to try and train my brain.

That chaos is not my home,
But peace feels so alone,
Awaiting dangers that seem inevitable.
Even in my nightmares, I have more control.

But here in the mundane,
Everything the same,
It strikes an urgent pain
That something must change.
This can't be my stage—
I have a bigger part to play.

But here I remain,
And in my sleep, I'll pertain
All the woulda, coulda, shoulda's—
If only
I'd stayed awake long enough.

10 Days

I'd like to introduce you to PMDD.
Ten days a month, my body fights me—
And every month, it gets harder to free
Myself from this hormonal banshee.

A quick list of symptoms,
So you can comprehend
A glimpse of my hindrance—
Then you might better apprehend:

It starts just after ovulation;
I start to lose motivation.

My hormones take me captive—domination.
Sleep for 18 hours—sedation.
Quick to anger—frustration.
Stomach pains—abrasion.
Skin breaks out—inflammation.
"Nobody likes me"—isolation.
Hate myself—defamation.
Suicidal thoughts seeking my termination.
You put it all together—it's quite the summation.

Life seemed so good two days ago—
Found beauty in the wind's gale
And the sun's glow.
Ten days doesn't seem far to go,
But each month, I escape by the tip of my toe.

Day eleven—I could take on the world.
Day ten—I'm a very different girl.
Shut myself away so no one knows,
And in my bed, I begin to decompose.

Too fatigued to clean my flat.
Beat myself up for not taking a bath.
On myself, I unleash the most wrath.
And I can't tell you what's up—
I'm just sad.

Yesterday, I saw light and hope.
Today, I fiend for the end of the rope.

The daunting I feel in anticipation—
Like a werewolf being tied up in preparation.
Write myself notes from me on brighter days
To remind me: these aren't my thoughts,
It's just a phase.

Even when I come out of it,
There's still a part of me that wants to quit.

Soon it'll come back round—
And again, I'll be fighting to stay above ground.

And then the dark thoughts really start to weigh in:
How could I ever entertain a relationship
When
I'm two different people? I wouldn't want to condemn
Them
To who I become—again and again.

Or how would I ever raise a baby
When for half the month, their mum's a different lady?

Right now, I'm only a burden to me.
But if I were to love someone so deeply,
I'd never put them in the disposition
Of having to deal with me in that condition.

And that's when I really start to lose hope.
Sure, I'll make it through the month, but it gets harder to cope.
Then I really start to spiral—
Sure, it's ten days, but it's an endless cycle.

Two weeks spent surviving,
The other two spent rectifying
Everything I neglected
When my hormones got hectic.

Feel like no matter what I do, I'm damned.
If life's a game,
I've been dealt a losing hand.

Right now, the future doesn't seem so bright.
But it's cool—
It's ten days.
I'll be alright

To Be or Not To Be

You've got a bleed on the brain,
and I felt some relief—
for the years of pain
would finally come to cease.
And I counted the vodka and champagne
that'd be needed for my party to leave,
and found solace in imagining how I'd be grieved.

You see, at the age of fifteen—
I set my expiration date.
To only make it to twenty-five seemed my fate.
From that point, the path I paved
became more and more depraved,
getting further and further from being saved.

And as my morals waved,
I found myself enslaved
to the notion
that my superpower was that I could not be broken.

But I'm no longer suicidal, doctor—
just occasionally, I don't bother
to look both ways before I wander
across busy roads with no bother.

To be or not to be—
That is the question.
A lifetime decision made in a split second.
Look in the mirror and ask my reflection,
"What do you reckon?"

Standing at the edge of the world,
and it's the final curtain call—
Do I stay or do I go?
Do I rise or do I fall?

One thing I know for sure
is that I'm ready to risk it all.
Either way, death is most definitely inevitable.
So, in the meantime, I may as well have a ball.

After the Storm

I feel like the storm's finally passed.
I want to be here—
And more importantly, I'm grateful to be here.

Reconnecting with God,
Finding a sense of purpose,
And now knowing my mission.

Even in the moments of hurt,
I give thanks that I have the capability to feel again.

I'm glad I chose to stay,
And I'm so incredibly proud of myself.
I put my trust
In my ability—
And in God's plan.

Chapter Two: A Moment of Your Time

For years, I've given advice—especially when it comes to healing and mental health. I even began using my social media platform to share my advice, in the hope it might reach someone who needed it.

My goal in life has always been simple: to help heal the world. There's something so beautiful about watching the weight lift from someone's shoulders after a conversation or helping them find a perspective that serves them better. That kind of healing brings me so much joy.

But for a long time, I felt like a fraud.
How could I speak with so much confidence when, deep down, I didn't even want to be here?

I've lived with PTSD, dissociation, depression, and anxiety since childhood.
Honestly, I was tired.

And when the darkness came, it made something painfully clear—these weren't new thoughts. I had been contemplating suicide every day.

Not always with the intention to act. It was more like... a twisted safety net.
No matter how bad things got, I told myself, *It's fine. You can always end it all.*

That mindset made me reckless. I never planned for the future, only cared about the here and now. And yes, that attitude came with a few "pros"—like not giving a fuck—but when it stems from a place of hopelessness, it always ends up hurting people.

I've never sought revenge on those who've hurt me. I've never met someone who was cruel to others and wasn't already cruel to themselves. I know this—because I was that person. And that, honestly, is punishment enough.

I still remember the moment everything cracked open. I was sitting at my dining table, writing a goodbye letter to my nephew.

Every part of me shattered.

The boy who lights up the room when I walk in. The one who saves me a seat at the table. My sunshine.

How could I ever let him grow up believing he wasn't a good enough reason for me to stay? How could I ever make him carry that trauma—the kind you never come back from?

In that moment, he was enough.
Maybe not forever. But enough to get me through the storm that day.

And then I picked up my notepad. The words spilled out like they'd been waiting for me all along.

That's how *A Moment of Your Time* was born.

I sobbed like I've never sobbed before.

I share all of this not for pity, but so you understand: I don't write from a place of distance or theory. I write from the edge. From the place I barely crawled back from.

I hope this book gives you the tools to never reach that point—or to never return to it.

But if you do find yourself there again, let this chapter stand as a reminder of all the reasons to stay.

A Moment of Your Time

Three…
Two…
Clock strikes midnight.
I'm finally twenty-five.
Double-check my pulse—
"No, this can't be right."
Heart still pounding,
"How am I still alive?"

Pick up my phone—
"Look, there's been an oversight.
I promised you twenty-four years
And you promised, then,
I could call it time.
I told you I was exhausted,
And you said,
"Just one last ride."

"No, you're not listening—
I'm tired.
I've got no more fight.
It's not fair for you
To not uphold your side.

Oh, and you won't let me cancel my subscription
To the strongest warrior package?
Well if there's no choice but conscription,
Then I will do the utmost damage."

The phone cuts dead.
Suddenly, standing beside my nightstand,
Stands a woman in red.

She says:
"Come, child—
Take my hand.
I've heard everything you've said,
And I understand.

But before you take your last breath,
There's just one last test.
If after that you still don't want to progress,
I promise, then, I shall lay you to rest."

Reluctantly, I take her hand—
We transport to outside my nephew's bedroom.
I say,
"He can't see us, I presume?"
She nods her head, and I hear a familiar tune—
He is winding up a music box I got him from Cancun.

Yesterday, he looked seven.
Now, he looks seventeen.
He's curled up on his bed,
Reading a postcard from me.

"My sunshine looks like he's lost all of his glow,"
She says,
"He never quite understood why you had to go.

Constantly asked his mum
If you were coming over soon.
And when she broke the news to him,
He didn't believe it to be true.
Waited on his bed for weeks—
For you.
Staring at his door,
Waiting for you to walk through."

Suddenly, it's as if he can see me.
And through gritted teeth,
He sobs,
"You promised you'd never leave me."

I fall to my knees
And begin to weep.
I look up at her and beg to leave.
She says,
"No—
There's more I need you to see."

She taps my shoulder and we quantum leap.

Just like that, we're transported to a living room—
And there's a man hitting a woman
Like a possessed baboon.
I try to intervene,
But my hand goes right through.

I look at her, bewildered,
"I don't see what this has to do—
With me."

She says,
"My child, without your words she won't leave."
She waves her hand and we enter a new scene.
This time, the same woman is sat on a cream settee,
And on her phone screen
Is a video of me.

She's watching so intently.
The red woman grabs my hand ever so gently
And says:
"One day, your words will impact many immensely.
Without hearing the fire in your belly,

She would've never been ready
To leave a relationship so deadly."

The red woman swipes her hand again—
But this time I see
The same woman left on the floor to bleed.

"But how is this fair?
Why is this my cross to bear?
I'm too damaged—far past repair."
She shields my eyes,
And then there's a bright white glare.

As she removes her hand,
Stood in front of me
Is myself—only fifteen.
She then asks me to repeat,
"I want you to tell her she can't be redeemed.

Tell her you're going to take it all away.
Tell her why she doesn't deserve to stay.
Tell her why she's not good enough.
Go on, tell her—
Tell her why she's too tough to love."

I stare into younger me's eyes.
As I do, she begins to cry.
On myself, I had inflicted the most spite—
And now, I had no place to hide.

"I can't," I replied.
The red woman then let out a sigh and said:
"To stay for others will keep you for a time—
But it is for yourself you must continue to fight."

So I dried younger me's eyes,
Pulled her in close and held her tight.
"I promise I won't give up on you this time."
And as we began to coincide,
There was a bright white light—
And just like that,
I was back to where I started my night.

So if you're seeing this now, it must mean it's true.
Sure, I stayed for me—
But I stayed for you too.
And that means it's not too late.
You're seeing this now, so it must be fate.

As hard as it may seem to cope,
You stayed to listen for a moment—
So there must still be hope.

So before you decide to leave,
If you can't stay for you,
Then please—
Stay for me.

jessica
Annty jess

Chapter Three: The Wounds I Had to Name

I've said in previous chapters how the darkness uncovered just how much had been left unresolved in my mind. I made a home in chaos because that was easier than sitting in stillness.

Stillness brought silence. And silence made it impossible to ignore the traumas I had left to lament for years.

I'd spent so long carrying around boxes I refused to unpack — dragging them into every relationship, every opportunity, every version of myself.

The first step was awareness. And the darkness forced me in front of the mirror and screamed, *LOOK.*

I had denied parts of myself for so long, because living in my truth felt shameful. Guilt-ridden. Dangerous.

But this *is* my truth.

If I were to tell the full story of my life by the age of twenty-six, it would be a trilogy at least. And maybe one day, I will. But for now, I offer you these fragments — told in poems. Because vulnerability breeds vulnerability.

And allowing yourself to be vulnerable is crucial to healing.
Vulnerability is a direct 'fuck you' to the ego.
It's a trembling but fierce: *"This is me — let me be me, so I can become a better me."*

Before we can reach accountability, we need awareness. And that, for me, is what the darkness taught me.

If you're reading this and still carrying boxes you've never dared to open — I see you. Maybe you don't have the words yet. Maybe you're not ready to name what hurts. That's okay.

Let this chapter be your invitation. Not to fix it all — but to begin noticing what still takes up space inside you.

You can't clean a wound you won't look at.

These poems aren't the whole story. But they are a beginning.

And beginnings are enough.

Genes & Queens

(Part One)

The thing that seems to get in the way of my dreams
Is my lack of self-esteem,
Lack of regime,
No routine,
No desire to be lean—

No gym queen
But I'm running out of steam.

Trying to pull at the seams of my genes
That have seen reams of screams,
Of queens who played to a theme:
Kids at sixteen,
Men that weren't keen,
And left them forever tinted a shade of green.

Never their scheme,
But they didn't leave the scene clean—either.
Fuck that. I've deemed it obscene.
I want serene.
I've foreseen the unseen.
Falls on me to redeem, intervene,
Find the vaccine—

Not for the sake of me,
But for who she'll grow to be.

Save The Tree

(Part Two)

I had to delve into my soul
To free my soul.
Mentally, that takes a toll.

But cycles—I've got to break.
A better life—I've got to make.
Future generations at stake,
But it's the risk I've got to take.

Only I can save me.
Guess that comes at a fee.
Gotta save the family tree—
My children,
I've got to free.

Mammy issues

"My mum doesn't like me,"
I would say as a teen.
Everyone told me,
"Stop being a drama queen."

For years, I thought maybe I was.
Always called too sensitive — too soft.

I still fear they'll leave,
maybe because when I was ten weeks,
she'd had enough of me
and decided to leave.
But before she abandoned me,
she told my father of her dream:
she hoped we'd one day pass on the street —
me not knowing her,
her not knowing me.

I still feel no one truly cares,
maybe because she was fully aware
the man she left us with had a nasty flare —
six years of torture,
and she left us there.

I still won't ask for help from anyone,
maybe because when I did,
I felt like a burden —
too much of a diversion
from the help she felt my siblings were
more deserving.

I still don't know how to be loved consistently.
Maybe because she
"loved all her children differently" —
a statement she made explicitly,
with not one ounce of sympathy.

I still chase validation,
maybe because I did anything for her attention.
Despite all my A's in examinations,
I was never given a congratulations.

I still doubt that I'm pretty.
Maybe because at fifteen,
she shattered my dream
when she said I didn't have the face for TV.

I'm still sensitive to rejection,
maybe because when I finally had the courage
to voice her lack of affection,
she told me
she never felt a connection.

I still shame myself endlessly,
maybe because she relentlessly
slut-shamed me for dressing "disrespectfully"
— though I had to learn it all independently.

I still meet conflict with dread,
maybe because when I fought back instead,
Without flinching she said,
"You'd be a terrible mother
It's a good thing your son's dead"

I still feel like I'm too tough to love,

maybe because —
if my mum can't love me,
then surely, nobody could.

I still run away,
maybe because she kicked me out at an early age.
If I leave before they push me away,
the price on my heart will be less to pay.

But.

I listen to the person at the table being ignored —
maybe because I've been that person before.
I nod, I stay, I reassure:
I see you. I'll make time for what you adore.

I make sure they don't go without,
maybe because I never got handouts.
I know what it's like to be in a drought
and still refuse to ask for help — out of pride and doubt.

I say "I love you" at the end of every call,
maybe because I know how it feels
to not feel important at all.
Even a line, ever so small,
can make someone feel ten feet tall.

I offer a safe space,
because I know what it's like
to be shamed, blamed,
ridiculed, erased.
I want them to know:
with me, they'll always have grace.

I nurture, endlessly,
maybe because I was deprived of that nursing.
But the cycle is reversing —
I'm learning I'm worthy,
I'm healing, I'm deserving.

I am incredibly kind,
maybe because I had my light denied.
Now I provide,
A space for people to shine.

I'll always long for a mum —
no matter the age, we never stop needing one.
But the mum I need isn't my mum,
so, I became a mother to those who have none.

Here Where Shame Lies

If only I had direction
When I was just a teen
To know a boy's attention
Was not a reflection
And would not boost my self-esteem

Upon further inspection
And a whole lot of introspection
I now know what mattered was intention
Prior intervention
May have been the prevention
As I now fear I'm past redemption

A lack of a mother's love was my deprivation
That sent me to stations with no destination
And although I'm now in a better location
I still carry the luggage of my past—
Shame, guilt, and fear of the wrath
For the things I collected on my path

As I try and set them down
And remind myself that the tools I have now
Weren't provided to allow
Myself to plough
The fields to sow
The seeds of love
In order to grow

The Looking Glass

The looking glass—
She'll do whatever you ask
If you're up for the task.
Easy to distract
As you bask—
In your own reflection.

But something grabs your attention,
Upon closer inspection,
Reveals a section
Left with no protection.

Chips that have begun to crack—
One fatal attack,
Smack
Or
Whack.

And everything you saw before
Crumbles to the floor,
Uncovering a corpse
Covered in spores
That she's absorbed from lovers before.

A judgment of error,
You didn't properly measure.
You sought a venture—
Sole objective: pleasure.

To your surprise,
What once seemed so nice
From the outside
Now doesn't shine so bright.

All lies to incite the right knight,
Willing to fight,
Willing to stride
Into a plight
That has left her denied
Of the outside.

Welcome to her humble abode,
Surrounded by once limestone,
Engulfed in flames and sand thrown,
Creating the glass walls you were shown.

Protecting the place she reluctantly calls home,
So it could remain unknown
That below her crowned throne,
She sits upon alone,
Is paved with fire and brimstone—
And cutting her feet to the bone.

What kind deed would you need to complete?
What kind of demons would you need to defeat?

To obtain such a feat,
All that is asked is that you lay down your sheath,
Place down a sheet
To lessen the heat upon both of your feet—
Halfway you could meet.

But she dare not speak
And tell you all that she needs
In order to be freed—
Choking on a weed,
Enwrapped in her teeth,
And causing her gums to bleed.

So, instead, she'll remain in her seat,
Watch you retreat
As you accept your defeat—
A cycle she's destined to repeat.

Chapter Four: Worthy of the Wound

By this stage, I had shed light on the wounds. I had named them.

I mentioned in Chapter One how, in the span of six years, I'd been in three abusive relationships. The truth is, I was so afraid of being alone, I would drink poison just to quench my thirst.

I was desperate for someone to save me.
And in that desperation, I refused to reflect on the cycles I kept repeating. So I met the same people — over and over — just wearing different faces.

There's a peculiar stage in healing. One that convinces you there's nothing left to heal. You feel emotionally intelligent, highly self-aware. But often, that feeling comes from one of two places.

Either we've become experts at avoiding anything that might trigger us — which can only last so long.
Or… there are wounds buried deep beneath guilt and shame. So deeply buried because, quite frankly, touching them *hurts.*

Because those wounds demand *accountability*.

Yes, many things have happened to us that we never deserved. But the truth is, people can only treat us the way we allow them to.

Owning that is painful. But it's necessary if we're ever going to break the pattern.

We also have to face the uncomfortable truth: that sometimes *we* have been the hurtful ones. Even the malicious ones. That we've been manipulative in subtle ways — through learned patterns and survival behaviour. Trying to "win" the game of connection, approval, or love. Often without even realising we're playing.

I became so obsessed with chasing validation from people who clearly didn't want me, that it drove me to places I'm not proud of.

How could they not see my worth?

I later realised — that desperation came from childhood trauma. When I was small, proving myself wasn't about self-esteem — it was about survival. If I didn't prove my worth, there was a chance I wouldn't be safe.
Maybe even a chance I wouldn't survive.

And sure — I have that awareness now.
But without *accountability* that I've carried that behaviour into every area of my life, I'd keep repeating it.

And then, you have to take accountability for changing your behaviour.

Because awareness means nothing if you're not willing to change.

Change doesn't come like flicking a switch.
These patterns are woven into us — stitched through our identity.
So we have to unpick every thread and say: I'm going to stitch myself back together properly — even if I wasn't the one who sewed this shitty hem in the first place.

This is where we re-build our foundation.

This is where we become *worthy* of our suffering.

This is where we stop being just products of our past. Where we start showing up properly. Loving people properly. Living properly.

And most importantly — where we become ready to receive the blessings that have always had our name on them.

Because you cannot receive what you do not believe you are worthy of.

Building self-worth has been one of the hardest battles I've ever faced.

If you had given me everything I once prayed for a year ago, I would've been so anxious something would go wrong — so convinced I didn't deserve it — that I'd have sabotaged it all and lost everything.

Only *you* can give yourself value.

> ***"There is only one thing that I dread: not to be worthy of my sufferings."***
> — Fyodor Dostoevsky

Accountability

How do I explain to the little girl crying,
Asking, "Did I do something wrong?"
That she did, in fact, do something wrong?

How do I tell the teenage girl, sobbing,
"I didn't deserve that,"
That she does, in fact, deserve what she accepts?

How do I break it to them
That, as the adult,
I failed—again—to protect them?

That I'll have to dissect both of them again,
To inspect what needs healing.

But that conversation can wait until tomorrow.
Tonight, I'll just hold them close and tight,
And let them know—
It's okay to cry

The 'How to Be Loved' Brief

She asked me to play shop
I said, "I'll try."
I handed her two breadsticks
"This is what I want to buy."

She told me,
"That'll be two times six."
I said, "Try and make sense of it."
She got frustrated and started to cry
I knelt and patted her tears dry.
"I don't know the answer," she sighed.
"Well, have you been shown?" I replied.

Her disappointed eyes met the ground and followed with a "No."
I gently whispered, "Well, how are you supposed to know?"

Her eyes softened with relief,
And something inside me began to grieve,
For I'd never received the 'how to be loved' brief—
My childhood stolen by a thief.

Too many times I'd tell myself
That I was the 'why' I got left on the shelf,
And too many times I'd carry the guilt
For boundaries I never got taught how to build.

A void in me started to fill—
A hole in my heart,
Realising it was never that hard.

"It's okay, I'll show you where to start."
And I picked her up and held her until
We both felt the world go still.
You don't need to know how to add up a bill

Or even know how to work a till—
Regardless, I'll love you still.

For you, my love, are not hard to love,
And you will always be more than enough.

The Sun Doesn't Abide

The sun doesn't abide
By your time to rise,
Nor does it seek permission to set.
I've embodied that mindset—
To no longer seek consent.
For it is their choice
To find peace or chaos in my sunset

The Price is Right

So, I used to go to this shop—right?
Open all day
And all night.

Twenty-four-seven,
My idea of heaven.

'Why you gassed?'
I hear you ask.

Well—
It's like they stocked everything for me.
Hard to believe,
But everything was free.

Absolutely no charge.
Even when I did try to pay,
They wouldn't take my card.

Got to a point where I was dependent on this free ride—
Because all my money would go on what they didn't provide.

Sure—
Sometimes I'd pay for what they'd got
At other shops.

But only 'cause it was convenient—
Then again, there was this one evening.

I popped down for some nourishment,
But they were closed for refurbishment.

Rumour was—
They were under new ownership

'Cause the last owner
Got them into a tight money sitch.

Now they wouldn't be open twenty-four-seven,
The new closing time would now be eleven.

Regardless, I returned a few days later,
But now they no longer catered—
To me.
It's cool though,
At least it's all still free.

Except—
When I went to walk away,
Now they're expecting me to pay.

'What do you mean?'
I've been coming here for years
With no expectation on me.
Now I'm obligated to pay a fee?
I only wanted half of this stuff 'cause it was free!

I demanded to see the manager—
'Look, I'm tryna fathom here—
Where did this all switch up?
You used to stock the finest of goods
Just to keep me hooked!'

That's when the manager replied—

"The exceptions we previously made
Finally took a toll,
And we started to lose trade.
Eventually we had to choose—
Was it you,
Or our business we lose?

And when we saw you shopping at other stores,
And having no problem paying at their door,
That's when it became clear
What we had to do—
We had to choose us
Because you'd always choose you."

Now obviously this story's not true.
To own such a store, you'd have to be a fool.
Imagine granting twenty-four-seven access to you,
And on your goods placing absolutely no value.

Truth be told, I used to be one of these owners.
Took me a while,
But I finally sought foreclosure.

Started to stock the goods I actually liked—
And because I actually liked them,
They were accurately priced.

Employed some security to keep thieves away,
Loyalty schemes to show real ones I appreciate.

Look, I'm not tryna preach,
But the lesson I am tryna teach
Is that:

People will only pay the price advertised.
So make sure you know your worth—
And never,
Argue your price

Good Girl

It took me years to master this calmness,
Years to harness
The discipline to smooth my tongue's sharpness,
To find kindness despite all that I endured in the darkness.

Incredibly understanding,
Put myself in the shoes they stand in.
Don't take it personal when they dish out their lashings,
And remind myself I'm not without sin.

I no longer shout and scream;
Instead, I've created boundaries,
Cut off those who don't align with me,
And have found happiness in my own company.

Created a safe space for others,
No longer envious of lovers,
More cautious with whom I share my covers,
And know there's more of myself to discover.

As long as I'm sweet,
Pleasant as can be,
Understanding,
Never angry —
Then I'm worthy.

Don't act out.
Don't shout.
Don't forget to count.
Shit.
I'm about to crash out.
No.
Don't make this about—
You.

No, fuck you.

You must've forgot who
The fuck I am.

Is that my ego?
I don't give a damn.
I'm tired of not acting human,
Only good enough if I'm a gentle woman.

I want to crash out,
And not have my love become in doubt.

I want my fire to rage,
And not be put back in my cage.
But rather they find beauty in my flames —
Not extinguish them or try to tame.

I deserve to be loved regardless,
To have light found in my darkness,
The same way I promised —
That when I love, I love in fullness.

I'm me,
In all of my duality,
Deserving to be loved fully —
When I'm a bitch, tired, or acting funny.

I'm me.
And I don't want to be your good girl
No more.

For the Man That Didn't Flinch

"It's hard for people not to love you,"
I asked you to repeat.
You said it again, ever so sincerely —
"It's hard for people NOT to love you."
And in a line, ever so brief,
I felt my biggest fear start to deplete.

There's no possible way you could've known.
To my chest, I hold it ever so close.
But coming from a person who knew me the most,
When the insecure parts of me had taken host...

And you —
Whom my daggered words have cut,
And me and my hands, laced with your blood —
Not once did you duck or rebuff,
Despite my constant uppercuts.

Not once did you raise your glove.
Instead, told me I'm human — and that gets tough.
Instead, told me I'm trying, and that's enough.
The fire in my fear, in one line, you snuffed.

That I am, in fact,
Not hard to love.

The Knight That Never Came

They say a leopard can't change its spots,
But she's not a leopard, and she's changed a lot.

In my bed, she used to leave me to rot,
Call me ugly every chance she got.

Neglect me of water throughout the day,
Constantly remind me of all the stupid things I'd say.
For my downfall, she would pray,
And list all the reasons for me not to stay.

Would highlight all my insecurities,
Constantly count my calories,
My weight she'd endlessly tease,
And tell me she hated me till I'd fall to my knees.

Leave the cupboards empty
So I couldn't eat,
Tell me all my friends hated me,
That I was the reason my ex would cheat,
And when I was cold, she refused the heat.

Told me I didn't deserve love,
That I'd never ever be enough.
There were even times my thighs, she'd cut
And tell me it was to toughen me up.

One day, I got sick of it —
Of every waking moment her giving me shit.
I told her we needed a conversation, and it's best she sit.
She started to cry and said she had some things to admit.

She'd only been cruel,
Because that's all she knew.

This was the love she'd been taught to pursue,
And no one had taught her the value of *you.*

It took a lot of work,
Of correcting her words —
When she'd try to hurt,
I'd replace them with kinder inserts.

Taught her my value,
It was hard, but I had to.
Took years, and I thought I'd never get through,
But one day, I saw her bloom.

I had reached a new low,
Couldn't think of who to phone.
Begged God for me not to be alone —
For someone to come and save me from this burning home.

And that's when she came to me —

"Come on, baby girl, you've got to eat."
"You deserve to live in a house that's clean."
"Just one more day, for me, please."

"I'll fetch you your favourite drink,"
"Come wash your face in the sink,"
"You're beautiful, despite what you think,"
"You're strong enough to overcome this thing."

"I got you some nice bath bombs,"
"I'll play all your favourite songs,"
"This feeling is temporary — it won't last long,"
"You're doing your best, and you're strong."

"Let's go for a nice walk,"
"You have friends that want to talk,"

"You've been through much worse than this before,"
"I know you're a good person at your core."

"Baby girl, you deserve to be loved,"
"You don't deserve to be judged,"
"You're trying your best, and right now, that's enough,"
"I know right now you just need a hug."

"Everything's going to be okay,"
"Look, here are 10 reasons to stay,"
"Let's dance — that always makes you happy,"
"You're human, you're allowed to get snappy."

"You're allowed to feel what you've got to feel,"
"If they run, then they were never real,"
"I'm proud of the work you've done to heal,"
"Let's sleep on it — and then see how you feel."

After years of her calling me a failure,
I never thought she could change her behaviour.
But in my darkest hour, she was my saviour,
And I wanted to do something to return the favour.

So I looked in the mirror,
And said:

Thank you.

Chapter Five: A Letter to The Girl Who Needed It Most

I didn't have an older sister growing up, nor a mum I could be vulnerable with. I was always too sensitive, too dramatic — made to feel like a burden. But the truth is: you never stop needing that guidance. I'm so grateful to have people around me now who make the time, who care more than enough to listen to my problems, offer advice, and hold space for me.

But there was a time I didn't have that. I didn't have anyone to confide in. No one to talk to about the way someone was treating me, or how I had come to believe I deserved it. The part of me that begged for the same man who once split my head open (twice) — to come home. To love me. To save me.

I wrote this poem for a few reasons. As a reminder to myself that there was a time, I prayed for things I wouldn't wish on my worst enemy now — and to remember that when I find myself being impatient or trying to force things that aren't meant for me. As a homage to just some of the things I've overcome — and to honour how incredibly proud I am of myself. And as a message to anyone who needs to hear it: there is no point living in regret.

Because if I could go back and save myself from all that pain… you wouldn't be reading this right now. So, whatever has come your way — whatever you're carrying — let this serve as a reminder: there is nothing you cannot overcome. Even in the darkest clouds, there are silver linings. Even in the darkest days, you are being shaped for something greater.

And most importantly — I became the person my younger self would have felt safe with. The one she would have looked up to. And that… is my greatest achievement.

Hindsight is a Beautiful Thing

Hi Jess,
It's me, Jessica.

If you could spare a few seconds,
I've got a few lessons
I wanna bless on ya.

By the looks of things, you're almost twenty-one now.
I can tell by the fresh scar just above your brow,
And how
This is the slimmest you've been.
I know food doesn't taste the same since him leaving—

'Cause you took beating after beating,
Every time you'd forgive him,
But he's the one who ended up cheating.

Convinced yourself—at least now he's found his next victim.
But I know
There's a part of you that can't help thinking,
'What's wrong with me?'
'Cause every day he called you ugly.

And his new girl's beautiful.
That can't be debated.
So maybe if you were prettier,
Your love would've been reciprocated.

Maybe if you wouldn't have seen that guy on the breakup,
Then maybe, just maybe—
He wouldn't hate us.

But baby—
None of that is true.
Being honest,

It was never going to work between you two.
I can see you hurting, I really do,
Picking apart all the flaws within you.

But you see—
The journey you're about to embark
Will see you find your once-lost spark.
You forgot how funny you once were.
And now?
Now—you're the main character.

You'll forget you were ever once shy,
And then you'll meet a real nice guy.
Six foot four—
The perfect height.
It was love at first sight.

Lockdown comes, so you move in.
Have you questioning,
'How the hell did I get him?'
So you'll push, and you'll push—
Just to get him to prove his love.

And baby—
Not once does he ever break,
Not once do his morals or values ever shake.

For years, you were taught love was pain.
Suddenly, you became the abuser—
And I still carry that shame.

A pregnancy came.
A pregnancy went.
A pregnancy caused you to resent.

Looking back, neither at fault—
And to be loved for a time still remains in my vault.

Now, the next few years wouldn't be so kind.
I'm not trying to scare you,
Please keep that in mind.

But, my dear, the worst is yet to come.
Because,
In 2022,
We would lose a son.

To a man that was incredibly cruel—
A man that went out of his way to pursue.
A man that sold us a dream—
A dream of a house, family, marriage,
And everything in between.

And when he had us in a place with no escape,
That's when the real him started to take shape.

Taking a beating was nothing new,
But it was his icy words that would cut right through.

To be made to feel so loved,
And then called crazy—
Honestly, that year still seems hazy.

But what I do recall—
Almost daily—
Was the day I begged God
To save me and my baby.

Out of our hands, it was took—
And just like anything, it came with a hook.

A blessing in disguise,
A blessing that came at a great sacrifice.

Between then and now—
There will be a few times homeless in between,
Some real evil men—
And I still don't feel quite clean.

Lose some friends that we thought were for life—
Some our fault,
Others just meaningless fights.
A few really, really dark nights,
A few attempts on our life.

Three years single and still alone—
But hey,
At least we now have a home
To call our own.

But now, baby girl—
Time for the hardest part.
I'm going to have to erase everything
I've told you so far.

No, don't argue with me—it's gotta be done.
I know I could save you all this pain,
Little one.
But then, I would not be the person
I've become.

It'll all be over soon, I promise.

Three.
Two.
One.

Hi Jessica,
I'm just a stranger,
But there are some important things
I wanna say to ya.

Firstly, my love—
You are not hard to love.
You have always been,
And always will be,
More than enough.

And on the day's things get really tough,
I need you to remember—
You have weathered
Storms much more rough.

The prices you pay on those rainy days
Are the deposits you make for better days.

So, in the meantime,
Give yourself grace.
And please, my love,
Be kind to yourself-
Always

Chapter Six: The Why Behind it All

I'll tell you later the biggest lesson the darkness taught me. Spoiler alert: a person with a why can endure almost any how.

In the depths of my darkest moments, I managed to talk myself down from acting on suicidal thoughts. Again and again. I'd claw my way out, moment by moment. But truthfully? I was still holding on by a thread. I had awareness. I had accountability. But I was missing something critical: purpose. Meaning. My reason why.

Everything shifted the day I stumbled across a book that would change my life: *Man's Search for Meaning* by Viktor Frankl. In it, he introduces logotherapy — a form of therapy built on the idea that life becomes bearable, even beautiful, when you have meaning. That even our suffering can be a source of strength, if we understand its why.

That book gave me the question that changed everything: *How could I be worthy of my suffering? What would make it worth something?*

And then it hit me. My passion — my poetry — is my purpose.

Why? Because through it, I get to help heal the world. Poetry is powerful because it invites, never demands. It offers a new perspective without forcing it. It gently says, "Here's something that helped me. Maybe it'll help you too."

With that mindset, I could finally see the gift buried inside all the pain I'd endured — and everything I'd inevitably go through. Every experience becomes a new lens to write from. A new way to connect. A new way to let someone know you are not alone.

Of course, our whys will look different. That's what makes us human. Your purpose may not be poetry — it may be music, parenting, building something, protecting something, standing for something. It doesn't matter what it is. What matters is that it burns in you. That it calls you back to yourself.

So, I want this chapter to be a spark. To make you ask: *What drives you? What makes your soul light up, even if no one else claps for it?*

Because fuck what anyone else wants for you. As cliché as it sounds — we only get one life. And it should be lived for you.

Depression is sometimes your body's way of saying: *"We don't want to live this life anymore."* So, ask yourself: *What is the life I do want to live? What is my why?*

This chapter shares some of mine — and how even the painful things have become part of my purpose.

"He who has a why to live can bear almost any how."
— Friedrich Nietzsche (quoted by Viktor Frankl)

Jacob

It's been three years since I gave birth.
This year, my heart hurts—-more.
Maybe it's because I've set aside the guilt to mourn,
Maybe because I've set aside the hate since you were born.

You know in movies when they're sat in the doctor's room,
And the patient spaces out after they break the news?
I can confirm that feeling is true—
Because that's how it felt when they broke the news about you.

For a moment, if only brief,
I'm ashamed to say I felt some relief—
Shame that weighed too heavy to believe,
That for you, I didn't deserve to grieve.

Your heart was growing in the wrong place,
A tumour was covering half of your face.
They told me I could have two weeks to contemplate—
I'd already started to feel you kick and
Couldn't bear the wait.

Rubbing my stomach, I felt my heart break.
To feel you and know I'd never hold you was too much to take.
A part of me felt this was better for your sake—
Easier than feeling guilt for want of an escape

Four months you were inside me.
Four months of being abused—it was hard to find
The experience exciting.
To be attached to that man for a lifetime was honestly terrifying.
But for you, I would've endured it all—there's no denying.

Three years have passed, and as I've grown,
I now know

I could've done it on my own—
Because my love for you would've protected you from any sorrow.

I didn't know if you'd be a boy or a girl
When I brought you into this world.
Your gender reveal was supposed to be the day I was in hospital.
February the 19th I lost you, and my heart's never been quite full.

February the 19th, I entered that room,
Knowing I'd leave without you.
February the 19th, I experienced pain I never knew—
But giving birth to you felt like the least I could do.

I was scared to look at you when you were born.
You weren't yet fully formed.
And I'm sorry, my baby—you deserved more from your mum.
But I went back the next day, I put you on my chest and held your thumb.

Born asleep, and I tucked you in,
Snuggled Piglet next to you to go in your coffin.
And your Auntie Holly always has your Winnie near—
Despite you not being here, we still hold you so dear.

I didn't cry at your funeral.
For a few weeks after, I was barely verbal.
I wasn't myself for a while and became hurtful—
Hurt that comes with not being a mother but being maternal.

It's a perplexing concept,
Not being able to pinpoint the upset.
How can I mourn someone I never met,
But mourn for what could've been instead?

For you, I would've devoted my life.
Perhaps that's another reason the timing wasn't right.
I'd be a different mother now, with all the gained insight.
It seemed dark for a while, but the future now seems more bright.

I catch myself in the baby aisle,
Tears streaming — but still, I smile.
Imagining all the outfits I'd style…
There'll always be a part of me that longs for a child.

Three years have now passed.
Although I'm still sad,
I've found gratitude in this alternative path,
And live my life twice as full—for the one you couldn't have.

So, I make this commitment to you, my love:
I'll devote living the best life I can, my cub.
Twice as full, to refill your cup.
You are my reason—my sweet Jacob.

I loved you yesterday,
I love you still.
I always have,
And always will

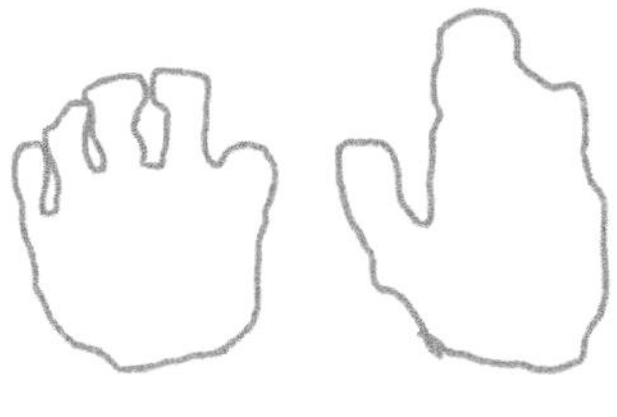

Jacob
19.02.2022

Rock of Gibraltar

Even in the darkest of moments, I have unwavering faith.
Faith in myself—but more importantly, in God.
Never against me, but for me.

Trust in God's plan for me.
Trust that I've got this.

Ask, and you shall receive.
Repent, and you shall be forgiven.

Move with only pure intentions,
And eventually, all will end in your favour—
Even if it doesn't feel like it right now.

Reach for His hand,
And you will always find it there.

What a beautiful God

Sparkle & Shine

My Nanna stands so tall at 5ft 1.
She's the reason I'm so headstrong,
Why I get angry at the morally wrong,
And why I refuse to sit at tables I don't belong.

Why I'm frustratingly stubborn,
Why I cannot be governed,
Why I'll never give in to corruption—
And why I know how to properly clean an oven.

My Nanna is no sheep.
She'll be the one to confront when others are afraid to speak,
Stand up for those who are weak—
And I've bore witness to the havoc she can wreak.

Her first grandbaby,
I carry her with me daily.
In everything I do, I can hear her faintly:
"Don't eat too thick pastry."

"Mean what you say and say what you mean."
"Nothing in this life comes for free."
"Trust your gut above everything."
"On your own head it shall be."

"Sparkle and shine"—
Is Nanna's favourite line.
And when I'm going through the hardest time,
I repeat it until I remember myself, and realign.

One of the strongest women I know—
A life that has seen a thousand sorrows.
Despite it all, every time she rose,
And her strength, in our family, shows.

So, when you see me sparkle and shine,
And wonder why I refuse to comply,
Or why I can make the best cheese & onion pie—
Just know: my Nanna's the reason why.

I love you to the moon and back.

While There's Still Time

I have an eerie feeling
That Death is on his way,
To take a loved one from me
To a place I cannot stay.

And of all the times I like to be right—
Today is not the day.
But just in case,
I'll treat it true,
And say what I've got to say.

I'll say what I mean,
And mean what I say.
Because
Tomorrow is never promised—
In any case.

Chapter Seven: Survivor's Gift

This is the chapter where the darkness begins to lift. And while I'm endlessly grateful to be standing in the light again, I carry with me the lessons that only the dark could teach. Because what's the point of surviving if you don't use what you've learned to help someone else?

I've spoken before about how isolating the darkness can be. How, even when you're surrounded by love, it can still feel like there's a wall between you and the world. There were times I couldn't reach out — not because I didn't have people, but because something inside me had shut down. And maybe, in a way, I needed to go through that part alone. I needed to learn, deeply, that no one was coming to save me — and that I had to be the one to reach for the rope.

But still... I often wished for a hand. A voice. A sign that I wasn't the only one. That's why I created this book. Not as a solution, but as a guide. A light. A quiet voice in the dark saying, "You're not alone."

This chapter is about what happens after survival. It's about choosing to share what we've learned — to turn our wounds into wisdom. To pass on the strength we found in ourselves, not because we have it all figured out, but because someone else might need to hear the exact words we once needed.

Because in the end, what is life without people? Without connection, without compassion, without the courage to reach back once we've made it out? That is the survivor's gift: to share. To say, "I've been there too." And to walk each other home.

Build and They Will Come

I missed community, so I built one.
God said, "Offer the table, and they will come."
They filled the table—and then some.
We broke bread and left no crumbs.

I cried that I had no village,
And God said, "Then build it."
So with straw and mud, I did it—
And they came to inhabit.

A weight too heavy on my chest,
And the Lord said, "Confess."
So to the table, I expressed—
Turns out we'd all been feeling suppressed.

I cried that I was alone,
God said, "Well, open up your home."
Gave each person a throne,
To bring light to their battles unknown.

I wept, "It's too dark out there."
And the Lord said, "Be the one to let off the flare."
In return, they each brought a chair
And their light to clear the polluted air.

I craved stability.
God said, "Provide the facility—
And let vulnerability breed vulnerability."
Our shared turmoil became tranquility.

It's not just you who craves the hum
Of friends indulging in wholesome.
It seems we all share the same gun,
All swimming in the same slum,

Against the same current,
All craving some fun
That doesn't involve clubs and rum.
So—
Build, and they will come.

In the Chaos, I Prayed

God,
I ask for your guidance, strength, and warm embrace.
Please calm my mind—
Give me health and respite
While these dark thoughts cloud my mind.

Allow me to see my errors,
And forgive me for my trespasses.
As I forgive those who have trespassed against me.

So I may be a vessel for Your work,
And help heal people.

Amen.

Please God.

In your glow, I basked.
Then finally, you lifted your mask.
To the floor, I collapsed,
And with the little air I could grasp,
'Please God' was all I could ask—
How am I to forgive this trespass?

'Please God' was all I could utter.
'Please God'—not another.
'Please God'—as I felt my heart rupture.
'Please God'—don't let me plunder into another slumber,
As I may not muster
The same courage as my tougher, younger structure.

'Please God'—ease my pain.
'Please God'—help me break this chain.
'Please God'—let it not be in vain.
'Please God'—assist me to train my brain,
So I can reign
Over my terrain,
And refrain from the temptation to entertain
The thoughts I once pertained.

'Please God'—I'm exhausted.
'Please God'—release the thoughts of them haunted.
'Please God'—let me not act on my thoughts so morbid.
'Please God'—in Your light, keep me supported.

And then I breathed real deep.
In exhaustion, I fell in a heap,
Fell into a deep sleep—
And that's when the answers came to me.

Because if it please God, I will not tremble.
If it please God, I'll rebuke the peril.
If it please God, I will not meddle, wrestle, or be vengeful.
And if it please God,
Instead, I will revel that He, ever so gentle,
Saw my potential,
And deemed me somewhat special—enough to be a vessel
To combat this devil.

When the world seems on a downward slope,
And everything feels a little too hard to cope,
If it please God, let me be a vessel to give others hope—
Those who are also at the end of their rope.

So if it please God, I'll take the weight of it all.
If it please God, to the pain I'll become enthralled.
If it please God, I'll get up after every fall.
If it please God, I'll answer His call,
And next to you, stand shoulder to shoulder,
Just as tall—
A reminder you're not alone after all.

I Still Sleep with A Night Light

Some people can recognise your light—
But can't handle the glare.
Others are scared
You're going to outshine theirs.

But some people
See your glow
As a guiding light out of the darkness.

So don't dim your light
To reduce their unrest—
Because you never know
Who needs your light
To make it through the night

My Hope Campfire

I have seen the darker side of life.
And I have confronted the shadows within me—
The ones cast by that darkness.

With only rock and flint, I sparked a fire—
Small, fragile,
But enough to welcome hope.

I nurtured that flame,
Tending to its flickers,
Until I became a beacon,
Guiding others
Out of their inherited shadows.

The only shadows here now
Are the ones we cast,
As we dance
By my fire of hope.

The Final Chapter: The War is Over-
Well at least this one is.

I didn't write this poem until the very end. Until the chapters were in place. Until I could see the full picture.
Because the truth is, I was still learning as I wrote this book — still putting pieces of myself back together. But something powerful happened while shaping each chapter: the journey became clear.

With every poem placed, with every reflection written, I realised just how far I'd come. I was starting to understand not only what I had survived, but what it had taught me. And I knew that if I was going to write something to close this — to truly close it — it had to come from the clearest place I'd reached yet.

By the time I wrote this poem, I had been in the light for a few months. I had steadied. I had softened. I had survived. Not perfectly, but honestly. And with that came the pressure — the kind you feel when you know something is important. This was the final poem. The finale. I wanted it to nurture. I wanted it to guide. I wanted it to hold space for anyone who needed a reason to keep going.

So I turned to my notebooks. My journals. Scribbled reminders I'd left myself throughout the year. And I gathered them all — the mantras, the questions, the lessons — and wove them into something I hope feels like a light. A breath. A beginning.

This isn't the end of my story — just the end of this chapter.
This particular war has been fought, felt, and finally, laid to rest.
And while I know there will be more battles ahead — because that's life —
I also know I'm not walking into them the same.

The war is over.
Well… at least this one is.
And I'm still here.

"I bathed in the flames that were meant to destroy me — and used them as fuel to be reborn."- Jay Pricey

What The Darkness Taught Me

Although the darkness almost took my life.
Really, it was a blessing in disguise.
And of the darkness, I'd like to shed some light—
on the knowledge I gained during that time.

So, what did the darkness teach?
That the hand we so desperately reach
is actually there at the end of our sleeve—
that we, ourselves, hold all that we need.

That the fear we feel
is really just worry that we cannot deal—
the stress we won't heal
when we're faced with the worst ordeal.

So feel the fear and do it anyway.
Despite the hundred thoughts that cause your mind to race,
despite the anxiety that keeps you awake—
I want you to hear it all and do it anyway.

That happiness cannot be pursued,
but rather ensued.
What does that mean to me and you?
Find something you love—and happiness will come too.

That real wealth
is knowing yourself—
enough to be able to tell:
Are these your thoughts, or the thoughts of someone else?

To slow down—there's no hurry.
It's about finding enjoyment in the journey.
You don't skip to the end just to read the glory—
The joy is found in the chapters of the story.

That self-love isn't just affirmations.
it's refusing to fill voids with temptations.
It's still loving yourself on the darkest occasions
and showing yourself incredible patience.

You won't get the most while doing the least.
Nothing worth having has ever come easy.

That I cannot keep
dragging boxes of trauma around with me.
I have to take accountability,
to do the work to become the best version of me.

In life, we won't always get to choose,
but we'll always get to choose our attitude—
to choose gratitude,
to choose peace over feud,
to focus on the more rather than the few—
That's when our blessings start breaking through.

That without knowing my worth,
I will continue to hurt.
You only accept what you deserve—
And it can only hurt if it hits a nerve.

That I had to do it alone, no doubt—
but community, relationships, and people
are what life's all about.
And the next time I sense the dark clouds,
I'll make sure to pick up my phone and speak aloud.

So, in my darkness, what did I find?
The power in having a why.
In the suffering, finding the silver line.
And here, I'll share mine:

Pain is new perspective.
Perspective is poetry.
Poetry is purpose.
And purpose is power.

The power to not just survive but thrive.
The power to stay just one more night.
The power to continue the fight.
The power to say, "I know I'll be alright."
The power to say, "and still I rise."
The power in having a why.

So, I ask you, my love—
What is your why?

The fire that burns in your chest to the right.
The fire that burns so bright
it could light
up the darkest of nights.

The passion that refuses to be denied.
The glow buried deep inside—
that, when found, becomes your guiding light.
That, my love, is where your why resides.

Whatever it may be—
art, music, people, or family—
hold your why valiantly,
and let your why become your rhapsody.

The darkness will come again.
Unfortunately, that is inevitable, my friend.
But let this darkness give you the tools to defend,
so, it never feels the same again.

I used to think my superpower was suicide.
Now, I know—
my superpower is my why.

So please, take my advice.
Let this all serve to remind:
even in the darkest of times—
everything, I promise, is going to be alright.

Chapter Nine: Behind The Poems

This chapter isn't here to tell you what the poems mean — that's for you to decide. I've always believed the power of poetry lies in what it awakens in the person reading it, not just in the person who wrote it. So, I'm not going to tell you what to take away from the work. But I do want to offer some truth about where I was when I wrote each piece. What I was feeling. What I was facing. What I didn't know how to say until the words found me.

I've loved literature for as long as I can remember. I've always found safety in words — in reading them, writing them, speaking them out loud. And I've always been drawn to the art of motivation. Something about helping someone shift the way they see their life — even just a little — that's what gives mine meaning.

But poetry? That wasn't something I ever planned to share. I didn't follow the traditional structures, and for a long time, I let that hold me back. I thought no one would take it seriously. I didn't think it counted. Until I realised that *raw* counts. That *truth* counts. And that the rhythm of healing doesn't follow a textbook either.

Most of these poems were written in one sitting. I write best when the emotion is high — when the feeling is fresh and pressing and can't be swallowed. If I don't finish a piece in that moment, it often stays unfinished. Writing, for me, is less about planning and more about catching a moment before it slips.

When I write, I try to keep George Orwell's writing rules in mind — not to sound clever, but to sound clear. Honest. Myself. I don't try to wrap pain up in metaphor if it doesn't need it. Sometimes, I just say it straight.

This chapter isn't analysis. It's context. A way to let you in on what was going on behind the page. A way to close the gap between poet and poem — not to explain, but to share.

Because even though I wrote these pieces for me, I'm sharing them for you.

When The Darkness Almost Caught me-
Behind The Poem:

I wrote this in the deepest part of the darkness. I've been broken before, but this felt like a new kind of break. I collapsed onto my carpet, clutching my stomach, rocking back and forth. Sobbing. Inconsolable. I felt like the end was near — and I couldn't figure out why. Why had this darkness consumed me so completely? It was as if someone had drained all the colour and hope out of the world. I usually romanticise everything. Find beauty in the mundane. But in that moment, I couldn't even remember that part of myself. It was like I was possessed. Like there was something lodged inside me that I couldn't name — and I wanted to rip myself open just to find it, just to get it out, so I could be normal. So, I could be better. I was terrified this was just who I was now: a broken person. So, I did the only thing I know to do when the pain becomes too much to carry inside — I grabbed my paper and pen.

Exhausted-
Behind The Poem

Exhausted was the first poem I ever shared under a pseudonym, back in the latter half of 2023. I had finally secured a stable home, stopped drinking, and started building a routine — work, gym, cooking, cleaning. I had been taught that this was the "good life." The *proper* life. But I hit a rock bottom. A different kind of darkness — not chaos, but a dull, hollow ache. A sense of *"What's the point?"* and *"Something's missing."*

Although it's not my strongest poem, it marks the beginning of an important realisation: that routine and survival aren't enough. That I needed passion. That I needed purpose. *Exhausted* was the first step toward rediscovering who I really am.

10 Days-
Behind The Poem

10 Days was one of the quickest poems I've ever written — 45 minutes, start to finish. I had set a challenge with a close friend, another poet, and just wrote what I was feeling in that moment. It was before I'd even considered medication, and I was deep in the worst part of my PMDD cycle. I was tired.

When I shared the poem with close friends, I realised how many women were silently suffering with the same thing. After I was diagnosed, I thought awareness would be enough. I prepped each month like battle — notes on my wall from happier days, gentle reminders that *"I promise you don't want to kill yourself,"* and treating myself like I would a child.

It worked, for a while. But each month, it got harder. And I knew I couldn't keep surviving like that.

This poem carries a deep sense of hopelessness — but I need you to know, this *isn't* just it. There are ways to ease the symptoms. It takes time, patience, trial and error… but it *can* get better.

For me, it got worse before it got better. But with medication, support, and persistence, I finally feel human again. Not perfect. Not "normal." But free. And functioning. And alive.

To Be or Not To Be-
Behind The Poem

Back in January 2024, just before I fully threw myself back into poetry, I was admitted to hospital with a suspected bleed on the brain. And I won't lie — a part of me felt relieved. I thought, *finally, it's over.*

I even found a strange kind of excitement in planning a "go away" party. When it turned out not to be a bleed, I was disappointed. That shook me.

It was a wake-up call. I realised I'd been manifesting death. Not through action, but through apathy. I made no plans for the future. I moved recklessly. I lived on autopilot, with no direction — just the quiet, passive hope that death would come and do the part I didn't have the courage to.

This poem was written from that space. The moment I realised that kind of hopelessness wasn't just haunting me — I was feeding it.

Genes & Queens and Save The Tree-
Behind The Poems:

I'm the first woman on my mother's side of the family to reach 18 without being pregnant. On that side, the "proper" path has always been clear — settle down, get a steady job, have kids, stay in a relationship. I was raised to believe that was the right way to live. And for a while, I played the part. I stayed in places I wasn't meant to be, in roles that didn't fit me. But the more I strayed from that path, the more distance it created between me and my family. They saw me as reckless, always met with comments like "you need to settle down" or "get your shit together." And for a long time, that resistance made me feel like a failure. Choosing healing made it harder — I struggled to be around them because it frustrated me that they couldn't see how their own cycles were hurting them. I knew I had cycles to break, but I also had to learn that it wasn't my job to change them. It was my job to heal the parts of me that were triggered by their resistance, and to stop taking it so personally. Because the truth is, I love my family. I didn't want to be apart from them. And with time — and without pressure — they started to embrace my path. They began cheering me on, bragging about me to their friends. I saw growth in them I never thought I'd witness. More patience. More understanding. More care. And all of it came from letting go of control — and holding on to love.

"Run to the rescue with love, and peace will follow." — *River Phoenix*

Mammy Issues
Behind The Poem:

I was hesitant to write this — guilty over how it might make my mum look. But this chapter is called *The Wounds I Had to Name* — and how could I not name the wound that's haunted me the most? My mother wound.

I've spent countless hours in therapists' chairs, sobbing over the simple truth that my mum couldn't love me in the way I needed. That she didn't protect me in the way a mother should. That I ended up in abusive relationships because the love I was taught wasn't love at all.

But this time, I didn't want to write from bitterness — I've done that before. I'm not angry anymore. I have understanding now. I know she's human. She was young. But this is still *my* truth — and I denied myself of it for far too long to protect her.

When it became clear that she had sacrificed me — repeatedly — for the sake of living the life *she* wanted, it was time I stopped offering her a courtesy she never offered me.
Still, I've chosen to preserve some of her dignity by not sharing every detail. That was a choice — for me.

I'll always need a mum.
But I've finally come to terms with the fact that — despite all my trying — my mum cannot be that for me.

And if you relate to this poem, I'm truly sorry.
This wound is one of the deepest. One that never fully heals.
But I believe we *can* learn to manage it. We can learn to mother ourselves. We can learn to build softer, safer homes in other people — and in ourselves.

Here Where Shame Lies
Behind The Poem:

This was the second poem I wrote after returning to poetry. It came from a conversation with a friend about the guilt we carried — and how we'd both been shamed by men for how we sought attention and affection when we were younger. We had never been taught that our worth didn't depend on who was interested in us. That validation isn't something you have to earn through your body or your availability. No one ever told me how sacred energy exchange is — in any form. That it's one of the most important decisions we make. Because of that, I spent years carrying shame and fear. Fear that I would never be truly loved because of the so-called "baggage" I carried. Because of the "numbers" I'd accumulated.

But while consoling a friend who felt the same, something clicked. I reminded her that some of us were simply *never taught* — and you can't know what you've never been taught. That conversation gave me the grace I had struggled to give myself. My past does not define me. What defines me are the choices I continue to make to grow, to heal, and to love myself better.

The Looking Glass-
Behind The Poem:

The Looking Glass is one of my few metaphorical poems. I wrote it after calling it quits with the first person, I'd ever truly felt a deep connection with. I cried for a week straight — not because of who they were, but because of what it revealed in me. I realised I had a pattern of running away or sabotaging anything that required real vulnerability. I also became aware of my tendency to mirror others — hence the title. I've been called a chameleon most of my life, able to shape-shift into whatever the person in front of me wanted. That skill had its benefits, especially in work, but it was destructive when it came to being loved for who I really am. In that moment, I realised it wasn't just unfair to the other person — it was deeply unfair to *me*. I needed to re-discover who I truly was beneath all the versions of myself I had created to be more likeable, more palatable, more wanted. Ironically, as I stopped trying to be what others needed and started being who I really am, I became more loved than I had ever been before. Not because I was trying — but because I finally wasn't.

Accountability-
Behind the poem:

Accountability started as a journal entry. You know that feeling when your heart physically aches? That deep, sinking thud with every beat? That's where I was. I had my suspicions about something — and then I saw the confirmation. My heart shattered. And to be honest, I think it's still under reconstruction. But I wasn't angry at the person. Technically, they hadn't done anything wrong. I didn't feel betrayed by them. I felt betrayed by *myself*. Because deep down, I knew. I knew I wasn't protecting myself. I knew how this would end. And still, I pursued it. I had to take accountability for the way I neglected myself. Looking back, accountability was absolutely necessary — but I no longer shame myself for how I felt. I was in love. And love, well... it's not always rational.

The How to Be Loved Brief-
Behind the poem:

The How to Be Loved Brief was one of my earliest poems. It was inspired by my nephew, Leo. One day, he broke down in tears because he couldn't figure out a math sum. He's always loved math's — definitely didn't get that from me — but this particular problem had him in pieces. He was frustrated, overwhelmed, and inconsolable. And I just said, *"If you've not been shown, how are you supposed to know?"* Instantly, I saw his shoulders relax. He realised it wasn't a reflection of his intelligence — just something he hadn't been taught yet. That moment stayed with me. Because I realised... it was the same for me. Not with math's, but with love. I had never been taught how to be loved properly — or how to love myself. The love I had experienced growing up wasn't love at all. But now I know:

It becomes so much easier to love yourself when you start loving yourself the way you love others. I'm so grateful that Leo will always know what it feels like to be loved fully — by me, and by his parents and our family. And in learning to give him that love, I started learning how to give it to myself too.

The Price is Right-
Behind the Poem:

The Price is Right was inspired by an anecdote I shared with a friend — about a shop that was open 24/7 and giving everything away for free. I said, "How could anyone take a shop like that seriously?" And the truth was — it wasn't the customers' fault. It was the *shop owner's* fault, for not valuing what they had. That story was really about me. About how we teach people how to treat us by what we allow. I could give that advice to others, but I wasn't living by it. When I sat down to write this poem, it was a reminder of the oath I made to myself: to *start taking my own advice.* I've said it before — only *you* can give yourself value. And once I started treating my time and energy like the currency it is, everything changed. I set boundaries. I became clear on what I could give and what I couldn't. I started respecting myself — and in turn, the respect I received from others was overwhelming. So let this be your reminder: know your worth, and don't ever argue your price.

Good Girl-
Behind The Poem:

Good Girl was written out of pure frustration — and you can probably tell. There had been a few moments where my boundaries were challenged, and when I reinforced them, it became painfully clear: some people only liked me when I was the kind, sweet, advice-giving Jessica. What they didn't understand is that the calm, peaceful version of me exists *because* I've learned to protect my space. I protect my peace so I can be a safe space for others. The part that hurt the most was realising I'd been glorified for my kindness — until I expressed limits. Suddenly I was "fake nice" or "showing my true colours." And that cut deep. Because when I love people, I love *all* their shades. I don't believe one shade is truer than the other — it's contextual. So I made a promise to myself: I will only share my time and energy with people who love and embrace all of my shades, the same way I do for them.

For The Man That Didn't Flinch-
Behind the poem:

For The Man That Didn't Flinch was one of the last poems I wrote before publishing this book. I thought I was so healed — until I met someone I wanted but couldn't have. They repeatedly told me that friendship was all they could offer, and out of fear of losing them, I agreed. But deep down, I knew I could never truly be just their friend. I would try, but every so often I'd spiral — and when I did, I'd lash out. I didn't even realise how much I was cutting them with my words. It wasn't malicious; I just couldn't imagine that I meant enough to them for my actions to hurt. But they stayed kind. Even after everything, they'd go out of their way to help me. They'd drop quiet lines like, *"You're hard not to love,"* even if they tried to play it off.

Eventually, I had to take full accountability — not just for my actions, but for the fact that I was becoming someone I didn't want to be. I became reactive, sharp, unkind — and that's not the kind of person I want to show up as, especially not to someone I care about. I had to accept that I couldn't be the friend they deserved.

I loved them enough to stay away.
And I love me enough to know I deserve a love that loves me back.

The Knight That Never Came-
Behind the poem:

The darkness taught me a lot, but one of the most important things it taught me was what self-love really is. I wanted this poem to capture just how unkind we can be to ourselves — in ways we don't even notice. It's easy to get angry thinking about someone treating a loved one the way the speaker is treated at the start of the poem. But it took me a long time to realise that person was *me.* I was the one treating myself that way. I didn't recognise it as abuse — until I had to learn how to truly love myself. And self-love wasn't just daily affirmations or nice words. It was acceptance. It was saying, "Okay, I might not be my best self today — but I still deserve love." It was learning to treat myself like I would treat someone I care about. It meant trusting that I'm not lazy or broken — that if something bothers me, it's because I care, and that's enough. It's believing that I have my own best intentions at heart. And on the days where I say, "not today," I give myself the same kindness I'd give to someone else. When we truly learn to love ourselves, it sets the bar for how we expect others to love us. I truly believe how you treat yourself reflects how you treat others. And I hope this poem offered a shift in perspective — a reminder to be kinder to yourself, always.

Jacob-
Behind the poem:

It was approaching the third anniversary of losing my son, Jacob. I've touched in previous chapters and poems on the abuse I suffered at the hands of Jacob's father. I had experienced an abusive relationship before and assumed that one was narcissistic — but I had no idea how much worse it could get. When I fell pregnant with Jacob, the relationship was already tumultuous. And despite the fact that my biggest wish in life has always been to be a mother, I felt deep down that going through with the pregnancy wasn't the right decision.

Before the pregnancy, there were several occasions where he would suffocate me to the point I thought, *this is it. I'm going to die.* And when I tried to leave, he would threaten to kill himself. He isolated me — turning the people around me against me. This was a man who had pursued me, created a fairytale, and then slowly started tearing it all away. And being completely honest, it was his coldness — his cutting words — that hurt more than the physical abuse ever did. Those wounds take much longer to heal.

Despite my hesitation, he convinced me to continue with the pregnancy. He told me he feared he couldn't have children, and promised he would change. That he would go back to being the person I fell in love with. And that's all I wanted — for things to go back to how they were. He told his entire family about the pregnancy, locking me into a decision. And then he became more abusive and more cold than ever before. He had me trapped, with no way out.

Before I was pregnant, I had been binge drinking — trying to numb the sadness of the situation I was in. I'd wake up crying about the relationship, and my solution was to get drunk again. When I got pregnant, the alcohol stopped — and with it, the illusion. I could no longer pretend the relationship wasn't destroying me.

I remember it vividly. I was parked up in my car, sobbing, praying to anyone who would listen — asking them to save me and my baby. Two days later, I went in for my dating scan. I was further along than I'd thought — sixteen weeks. The midwife had me lie on my side, roll over, go for a walk, try different positions. I knew something wasn't right.

A further scan was booked a week later. One of the hardest weeks of my life.

They told me Jacob had a tumour growing over his mouth and nose, and his heart and brain were developing in the wrong place. The world stopped. And for full transparency — because I deserve to live in my truth — my first reaction was relief. This wasn't a world I wanted to bring my child into. And selfishly, it wasn't a world I wanted to stay in either.

It was made clear that it would take a miracle for me to make it full term never mind Jacob surviving the birth. I didn't want my baby to suffer so the decision was clear.

A week later, I gave birth to Jacob. And because of that relief, I felt like I didn't deserve to grieve. But writing this poem helped me do just that. It gave me space to reflect, to cry, and to truly mourn my son. I know now that I *would* have made it work as a single mother. I would have been an incredible mum to Jacob. But I also know I would be a very different mother now than I would have been back then.

My path was shifted. That wasn't the life meant for me. But I made a promise to myself that I would live a life that honours that detour. That I would take full advantage of the opportunities I've been given on this different path — and that Jacob's memory would live on in everything I create.

Sparkle & Shine-
Behind the poem

Sparkle & Shine was written for my Nanna's birthday. As I've touched on before, she had custody of me as a baby, and when we were reunited, we became inseparable. My Nanna has been like a mum to me. She took me in after I lost my son and gave me multiple chances when my behaviour turned destructive in the aftermath of that grief. At the time, I couldn't see the damage I was causing — I just felt like I was being picked at. But no matter how many times I snapped, it was nothing a cuddle and a sorry couldn't fix. I took my frustrations out on my Nanna because she was the safest place I had — and she knew that. That doesn't excuse it.

Despite everything, she still got up early to iron my suit for big work events, and every time I left the house, she'd say, *"Sparkle and shine."* Then she'd remind me: *"You're a sparkle and shine kind of girl."*

As I healed, I began to understand just how much my Nanna has lived through. I saw the strength it took for her to raise a family, the sacrifices she made quietly, and the ways that hardship can leave wounds of its own. Wounds I used to take personally. But when I became more considerate and open-hearted toward her pain — when I simply acknowledged it — something shifted between us. She began to meet me with that same understanding.

I love my Nanna deeply. I understand the sacrifices she's made. And that's why I'm determined to honour them — by living my life to the fullest and carrying her strength with me in everything I do.

While There's Still Time-
Behind the poem:

While There's Still Time was written in a moment of fear — the kind that grips all of us when we imagine losing someone we love. I took the time to really sit with that fear. What was it that scared me most? Was it the thought of losing them… or the thought of them leaving this world without knowing just how much they meant to me?

Of course, I want the people I love to be here forever. But death is inevitable. That part is out of my control — and I refuse to fear what is out of my control. What *is* in my control is making sure they never have to question how deeply I love them. To remind them — in every form I can — how much they matter.

Honestly, this poem could have slotted into many chapters.

But I chose to place it here — because this is just another one of my *whys.*

I placed this poem here, and even wrote this Behind the poem two weeks before my stepdad passed. How easy it was to say, 'I refuse to fear anything out of my control'. I had never lost someone so close to me, especially without being able to say goodbye. And that awoke a fear in me to ensure that I always kept this poem in mind, in everything I do. To hold my loved ones a little tighter, to tell them a little louder how much I love them. It still remains that this *is another one of my whys.*

But after the tragic loss of my stepdad, Simon, it holds so much more weight to me now.

I love you Si. Wherever you are, I pray I've done you proud.

Build and They Will Come-
Behind the poem:

This poem was written just as I was coming out of the darkness. I wanted to celebrate something that, honestly, felt massive to me — that I was still here. Still alive. Still standing. So, I decided to gather some of my friends. No big occasion, no birthday, no reason other than to share food and good energy. I missed connections that didn't involve clubs or chaos. So, I created it.

There were ten of us. Everyone brought food. We played a card game called *I Can't Afford Therapy* — which sparked conversations about things most of us had never shared. I heard people I've known for years say things I never knew they were holding. It was like we all took a deep breath together. We saw each other in new ways. And it made one thing clear: so many of us are struggling, and so few of us are saying it out loud.

By the end of the night, we were caught in a loop of mutual gratitude — me thanking them for coming, them thanking me for holding the space. None of us had realised just how much we needed it. This poem is a tribute to that night, to that community, and to the divine reminder that if you build the space — with love, with intention — they will come.

Author's Final Note

If you've made it this far — firstly, thank you. Truly. Thank you for sitting with my words, for holding space for parts of me that even I once found hard to sit with. I didn't write this book just to share poetry. I wrote it because I didn't want anyone else to feel as alone as I once did. I wrote it for the version of me that didn't have the language yet. For anyone who needed something real to hold onto.

Selfishly, this book has also been a way for me to close the door on a lot of chapters in my life. It became a kind of baby to me — my project. Something so raw and vulnerable that I started to doubt whether I should even share it with the world. I was scared it wouldn't offer anyone anything but me trauma-dumping. But I've come to realise: those few seconds before we take the leap — that's when it's the scariest. What's waiting on the other side can't be guaranteed. But what *is* guaranteed, is that if you don't leap, you stay exactly where you are. I'm glad I found the courage to share this. And I hope, even if it's just the smallest glimpse — it's offered you some light.

Healing isn't a straight line. It's messy. It's layered. It's learning, slipping up, forgiving yourself, and choosing to try again. I'm not the same person I was when I wrote these poems, and I won't be the same person next year. That's what growth is — letting yourself change, letting go of shame, and making space for grace.

The darkness taught me a lot. But I'm still learning.

And if this book reminded you that you can too — then it's done what I hoped it would.

"You clearly want to make some shit, so why not just make it?"
— Tyler, The Creator

Hear It Spoken

If you'd like to experience these poems in spoken word form, you can find me here:

YouTube: [@Jay.Pricey]
TikTok: [@xjaypriceyx]
Instagram: [@xjpriceyx]

Your support means the world — thank you for listening.

Acknowledgements

First and foremost, to my little sister Holly — my rock, my cheerleader, my inspiration. Everything I have worked for has been to become the best version of myself for you, to be the role model you deserve, and, of course, to earn that all-important teenage validation from you and your friends. I hope my journey inspires you to chase your own greatness.

To Jade- my sissy, My Robin. There is a certain darkness that only we endured and that only we will know. We didn't deserve that darkness, we were only little girls. But I would live it a thousand times over to ensure that I was there to protect you the best a child could. I hope this book provides proof to you that there is power in what we went through and one day you will join me in the light.

To Daniel- my little brother, I want you to know no matter the time or the distance you will always hold a special place in my heart. I am only ever a phone call away. I'm so proud of you and love you.

To Tyler- I've had the honour of watching you grow from the very beginning. From your first steps to the person you're becoming, it's been a joy to witness your journey. You're growing into such a respectful, kind-hearted young man, and I couldn't be prouder of you.

To Teonna — my best friend with a heart of gold. I would never have survived high school years without you (or your mum, who would always make sure I always felt included). Thank you for laughing at all my jokes and reminding me of my light, even when I couldn't see it myself.

To Elisha — I am so incredibly proud of you. You never sugarcoat the truth, always keep it real, and hold me accountable when I need it most. I'm grateful for your loyalty and your honesty.

To Amelia — thank you for blessing me with your emotional intelligence and always keeping it real.

To Angel —my light, my mentor. I never had a big sister, but you taught me what it's like to have one. In my darkest moments, you pulled me out time and time again. You are one of the very few people I feel completely safe with, and one of the strongest women I know. To your beautiful daughter Cordelia — you are already a force to be reckoned with, and I can't wait to see the incredible woman you grow to become.

To Kayleigh — thank you for always be there, checking in on me- and never getting offended by my lack of response. I truly appreciate you

To Mia- thank you my love, for always taking the time to listen to me and reassuring me just how great of a human I am. I miss you dearly but it makes me so happy that you are living your best life.

To Rach — thank you for always lending a non-judgmental ear, cheering me on, and reassuring me when I needed it most.

To Ashleigh and Michael — for always being in my corner and giving me the greatest nephews a girl could ask for.

To Nanna and Grandad — thank you for your patience while I was still learning to be my best self, and for always being so eager to celebrate my wins, big and small.

To Grandad Mac- thank you for always cheering me on, being the proudest Grandpapa and looking after Holly so well.

To Aunty Tracy- thank you for teaching me unconditional love is, always cheering me on and reminding to be unapologetically myself

To My Pops- for being the best dad you can be despite the barriers put up against you and the gift of poetry I inherited from you

To King Kari — more than a friend, a brother. Thank you for giving me the rare gift of a safe space to cry, for the countless hours spent listening to my heart break and helping me piece it back together. We win together.

To Nash — for pushing me to chase my passions and always reminding me of my worth. Your honesty and support have meant the world.

To Remel- thank you for always checking in on me, giving me the space to vent and reminding me of my power

To Roukaya — thank you for being a supportive friend whether I'm struggling or winning. For being a safe space when my anxiety gets the better of me and safe space for me to be completely myself. Your authenticity gives me the courage to be unapologetically myself too.

To Cronica — thank you for always cheering me up and finding a way to connect everything back to superheroes. You have a truly special gift.

To Kiz —an artistic genius. Thank you for understanding my visions and bringing them to life so beautifully.

To Yasi — thank you for the time you empowered me when I couldn't find my power

To Layla— it's been an honour to witness your greatness you will go on to achieve even greater things.

To Sadiq — thank you for your honesty, accountability, and the conversations that have stayed with me.

To Jack A- thank you for believing in me when I didn't believe in myself and for top tier banter.

To Ethan- the best chef I know. Thank you for always making sure we're all well fed, taking care of me and offering me one of the few spaces where my minds at peace.

To Oggy- thank you. I would've never achieved all that I have without your guidance and patience when I was still finding my feet as a troubled twenty-year-old. Thank you for not giving up on me, picking up my disaster calls at the most inconvenient times and listen to me chat nonsense on our wanders.

To Louise — the most incredible manager and mentor. You reminded me to put myself first and gave me the space to grow. I would not be the person I am today without your guidance.

To Maria — thank you for seeing my potential before I even saw it myself and allowing me the space to blossom.

To Chris- thank you for bestowing on me knowledge that will serve me great purpose throughout my journey.

To Eleri — thank you for cheering me on, mentoring me, and inspiring me to be an unapologetically strong woman who takes no shit. I want to be like you when I grow up.

To Ajufa — my work bestie. God knows you kept me sane!

Sarah- thank you for always providing the brief 5 minutes in my workday to breath and feel like a human. I appreciate you more than you know.

To Loz- for always being extra caring and looking out for me in work. It's truly appreciated.

Trevor- thank you for always brightening my day up in work and offering me fatherly guidance. Whether I want it or not.

Jonathan (JP) - thank you for giving me a safe space to find ways to hold myself accountable. The advice and guidance you gave was life changing and I carry it with me in everything I do.

Oldham Council staff- thank you to all those who have contributed to my growth, given advice and added to my love for my job. My love for Oldham stems from the great staff I have encountered at Oldham Council

Tommyfield Market & Market Team- In my darkest moments, coming into the market & office was the highlight of my day. From banter with the traders to debates in the office. It provided light in the darkness.

To Cerys- thank you for offering me a home when I didn't have one and more importantly a shoulder to cry on. I will forever be indebted to you

To Ewan- thank you for taking the time and energy to put together my book cover, you brought my vision to life beautifully.

To DJ- thank you for always lending an ear to listen to the thousand things racing my mind and reminding me the real family is the one we choose.

To J — thank you, unbeknownst to you, for being a muse, motivator, mentor, and master. You mean more to me than you'll ever know. I only wish I could have been a friend to you.

And to Leo — my sunshine. My nephew. You are too young now to understand the depth of what these pages carry, and I pray you never have to walk through the kind of darkness that inspired them.

I didn't write this book for you to need — I wrote it just in case. But if you ever do, know this: it was your light that saved me.

You are, and will always be, one of my greatest reasons to keep choosing the light. I carry you with me in everything I do.

To all those that I've met on my journey. Whether we have been separated through distance or conflict. I keep you in my prayers and carry the fragments of our connections with me in all I do- positive or negative I value the lessons. Thank you for the time we shared together.

To everyone who ever took the time to listen to me or my poetry, to watch me perform, and to support and cheer me on — thank you. You have no idea how much your love has carried me.

This book is for all of you.

And finally, to God- I give thanks for all the blessings, lessons, strength and patience you provide me with. I could not do this without your guidance and forgiveness.

My Love, everything is going to be okay- I promise.